STAR WARS™

POSTE

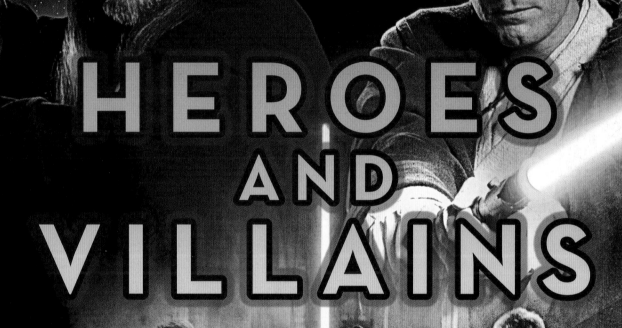

HEROES AND VILLAINS

Time Inc. Books

Publisher Margot Schupf
Associate Publisher Allison Devlin
Vice President, Finance Terri Lombardi
Executive Director, Marketing Services Carol Pittard
Executive Director, Business Development Suzanne Albert
Executive Publishing Director Megan Pearlman
Associate Director of Publicity Courtney Greenhalgh
Assistant General Counsel Andrew Goldberg
Assistant Director, Special Sales Ilene Schreider
Assistant Director, Finance Christine Font
Assistant Director, Production Susan Chodakiewicz
Senior Manager, Sales Marketing Danielle Costa
Senior Manager, Children's Category Marketing Amanda Lipnick
Senior Manager, Business Development and Partnerships Nina Fleishman Reed
Manager, Business Development and Partnerships Stephanie Braga
Associate Project Manager Amy Mangus
Associate Prepress Manager Alex Voznesenskiy

Editorial Director Stephen Koepp
Art Director Gary Stewart
Editorial Operations Director Jamie Roth Major
Senior Editor Alyssa Smith
Editor, Children's Books Jonathan White
Copy Chief Rina Bander
Design Manager Anne-Michelle Gallero
Assistant Managing Editor Gina Scauzillo
Editorial Assistant Courtney Mifsud

SPECIAL THANKS TO
Allyson Angle, Curt Baker, Brad Beatson, Jeremy Biloon, Ian Chin,
Rose Cirrincione, Pat Datta, Alison Foster, Erika Hawxhurst, Samantha Holland,
Kristina Jutzi, David Kahn, Jean Kennedy, Hillary Leary, Kimberly Marshall,
Melissa Presti, Babette Ross, Dave Rozzelle, Divyam Shrivastava,
Larry Wicker, Krista Wong

Produced by DOWNTOWN BOOKWORKS INC.

President Julie Merberg
Editorial Director Sarah Parvis
Editorial Assistant Sara DiSalvo
Editorial Intern Laura Petro
Cover and Interior Design Georgia Rucker
Writer Michael Robin

Published by Time Inc. Books
1271 Avenue of the Americas, 6th floor • New York, NY 10020

ISBN 10: 1-61893-400-7
ISBN 13: 978-1-61893-400-0

We welcome your comments and suggestions about Time Inc. Books.
Please write to us at:
Time Inc. Books
Attention: Book Editors
P.O. Box 361095
Des Moines, IA 50336-1095

If you would like to order any of our hardcover Collector's Edition books, please
call us at 800-327-6388, Monday through Friday, 7 a.m.–9 p.m. Central Time.

1 QGW 15

At first it seemed so easy: the bad guy wore black. He even *breathed* scarily. But we soon found out that the man in black used to be a hero. And, before our eyes, he became a hero again. Keeping track of *Star Wars* heroes and villains can be tricky business!

The Jedi Knights stand for the noblest ideals. Smugglers look out only for themselves. Yet it was a fallen Jedi who brought on the evil Empire and a smuggler who helped bring it down.

On the following pages are the *Star Wars* heroes we love to cheer and the *Star Wars* villains we love to. . . well, to be honest, we usually cheer them too.

Every page can be cut out and hung up as a poster. Now strap yourselves in. We're going to make the jump to light speed!

ANAKIN

When I grow up, I want to be a Jedi.

YOU ARE A JEDI. YOUR YOUR WEAPON IS YOUR LIFE.

QUI-GON JINN

Trust your instincts.

You will
be a Jedi.
I promise.

JAR JAR

A HERO IS NOT MEASURED BY HIS TABLE MANNERS.

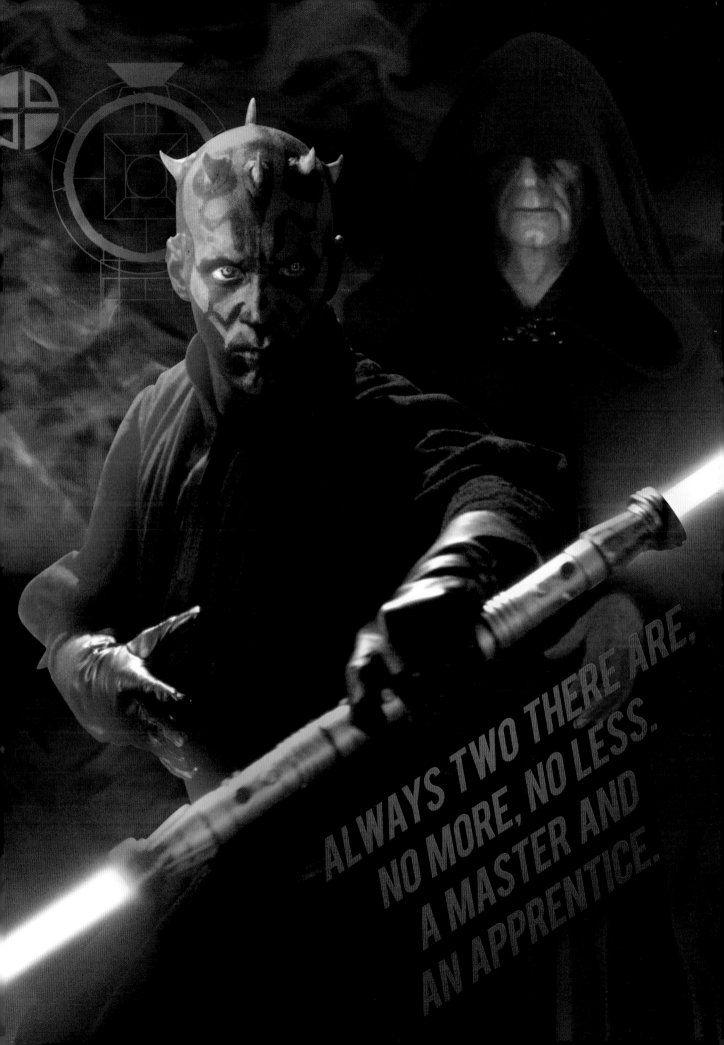

ALWAYS TWO THERE ARE, NO MORE, NO LESS. A MASTER AND AN APPRENTICE.

DARTH MAUL

Mind tricks don't work on me. Only money.

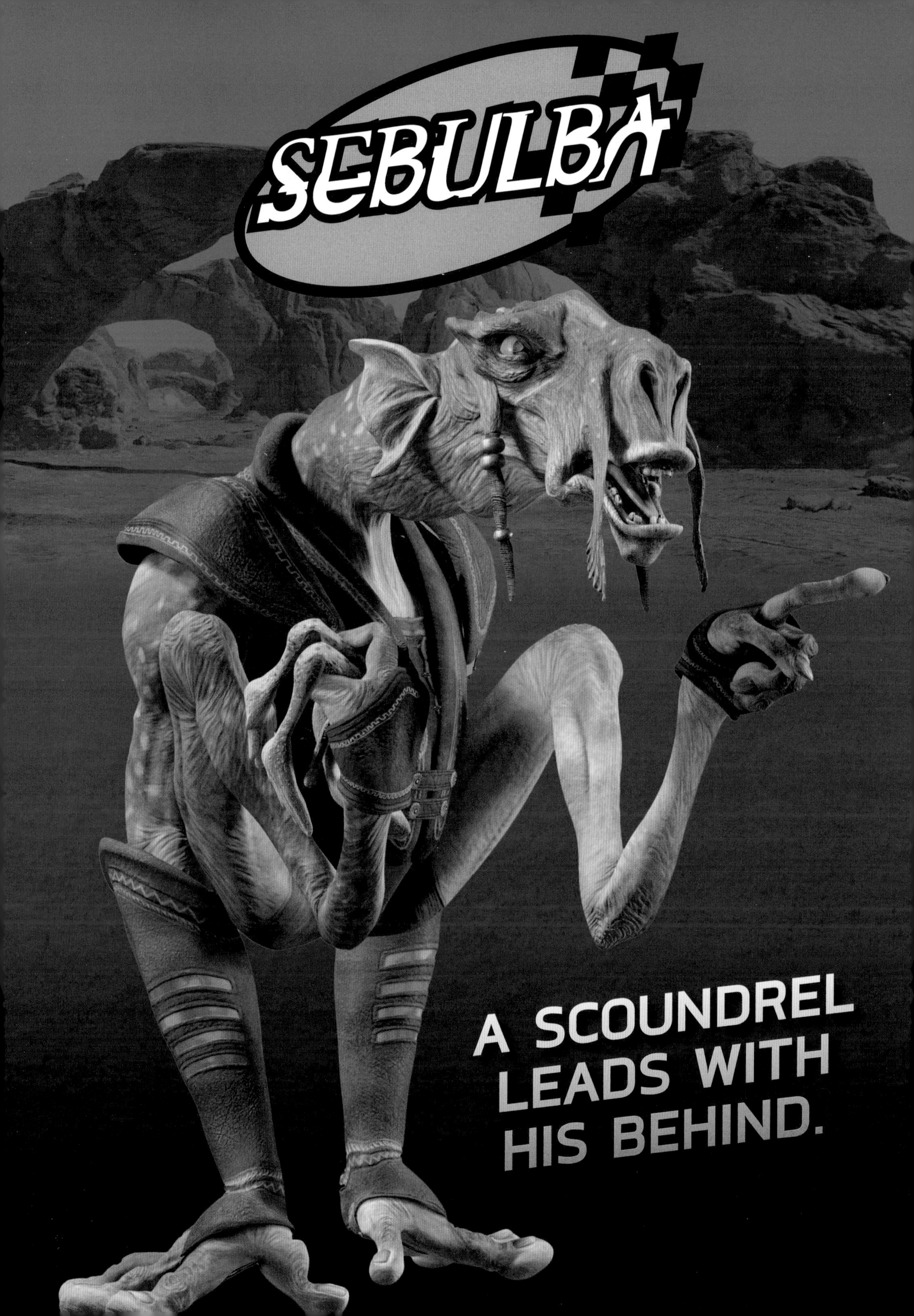
SEBULBA
A SCOUNDREL LEADS WITH HIS BEHIND.

GREED CAN BE A VERY POWERFUL ALLY.

REVENGE
IS THE BEST MEDICINE.

HEROES FALL.
CARRY ON.

ZAM WESELL

TROUBLE TAKES SHAPE.

R2-D2

RISE ABOVE
YOUR
SOFTWARE.

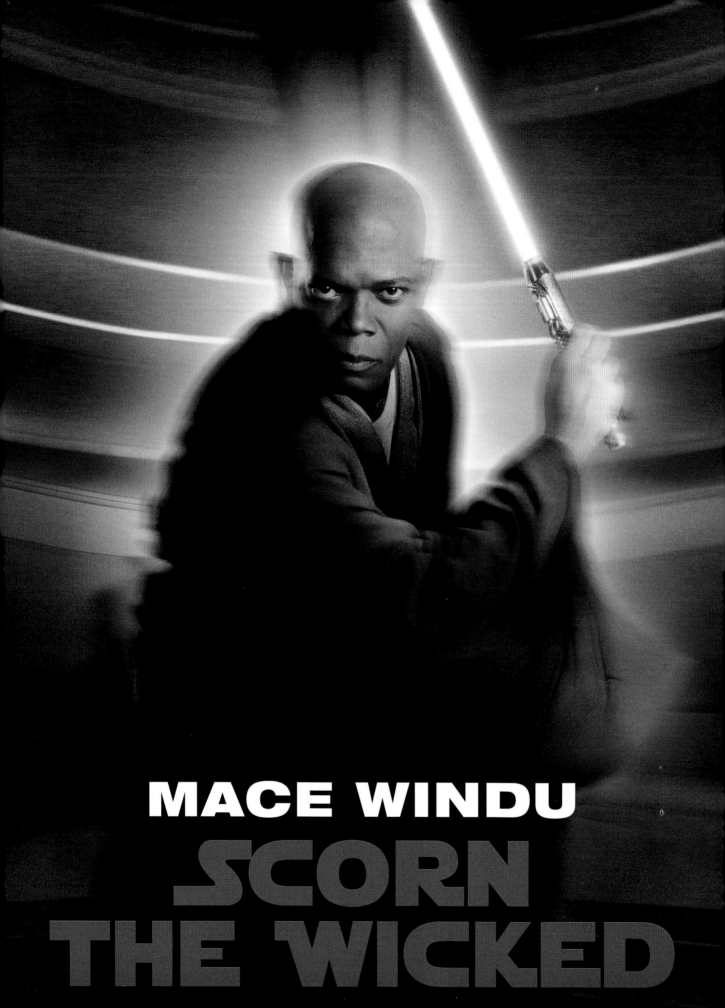

MACE WINDU
SCORN
THE WICKED

HEROES
STAND

TOGETHER.

CAUGHT IN THE CROSSFIRE

No politics, no plotting, no war.

BACK DOWN?
I DON'T
THINK SO.

PADMÉ
AMIDALA

READY FOR
AGGRESSIVE
NEGOTIATIONS

Outnumbered and Unafraid

JANGO FETT.
SO GOOD THEY MADE 200,000 MORE
WITH ANOTHER MILLION WELL ON THEIR WAY.

ROLE
MODELS
MATTER.

LIKE FATHER,
LIKE SON

COUNT DOOKU

SURELY YOU CAN DO BETTER.

It's all fun and games until someone loses a hand.

THE CLANKERS ARE COMING!

CLONE

HEROES
NEVER
GIVE UP.

Heroes come in all shapes and sizes.

EVIL IS PATIENT.

Armed & Dangerous

SENATOR
AMIDALA

Words end wars.

GOOD RELATIONS
WITH THE
WOOKIEES,
I HAVE.

Looks like someone woke up on the wrong side of the Force.

JEDI

THE GALAXY IS NOT ENOUGH!

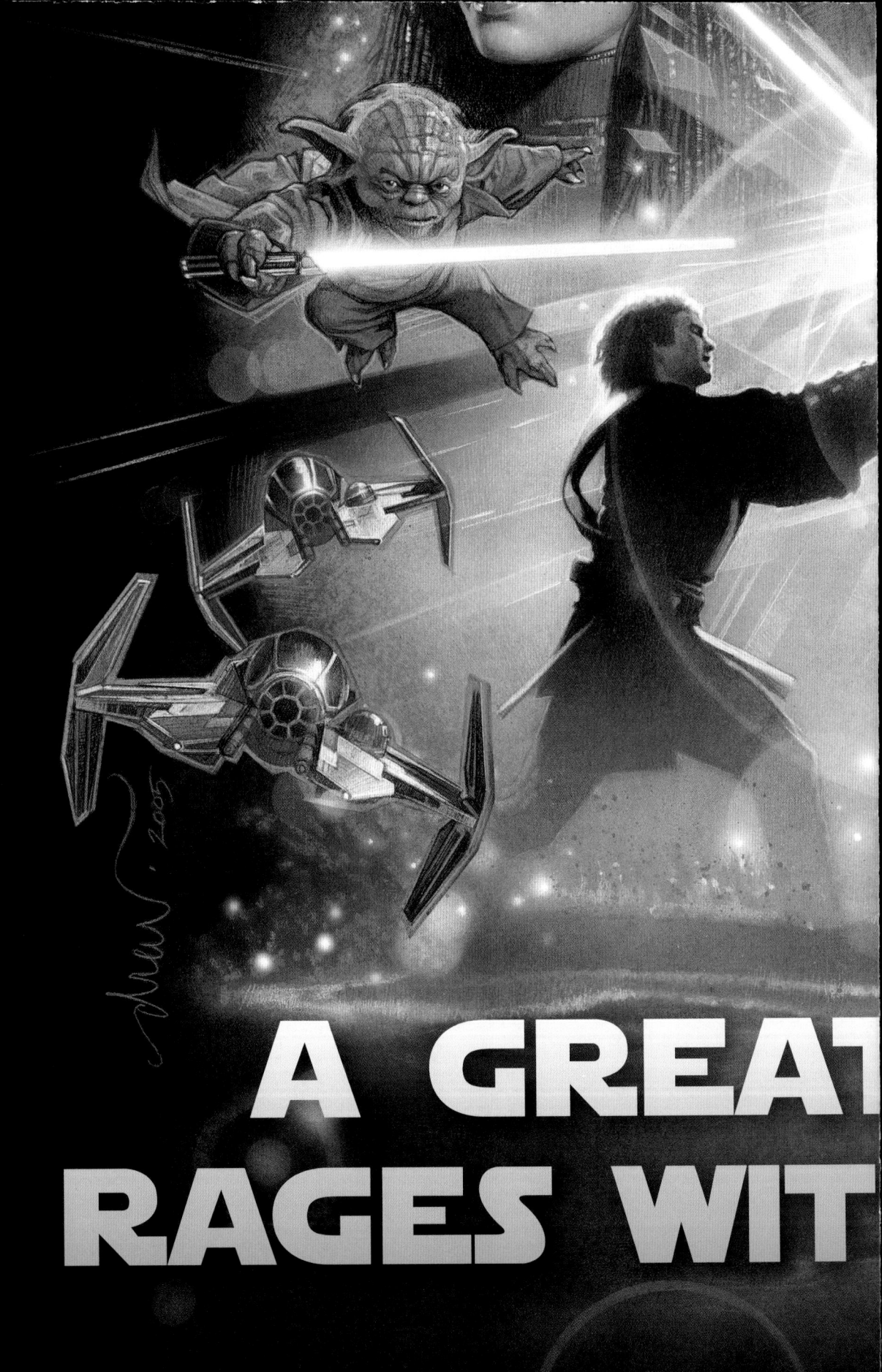

A GREAT
RAGES WIT

THE EMPIRE IS WATCHING.

SITH LORD

UNLIMITED POWER

VADER

BURNOUT

TRIAL BY FIRE

LUKE SKYWALKER

PRINCESS
LEIA

HAN SOLO

FEEL THE FORCE

If you strike
me down,
I shall become
more powerful
than you can
possibly
imagine.

THESE ARE THE DROIDS YOU'RE LOOKING FOR.

TALL, DARK, AND AWESOME

WANNA GO
FOR A RIDE IN
MY DEATH
STAR?

C-3PO

Don't blame me. I'm an interpreter.

THERE'S ALWAYS ANOTHER WAY OUT.

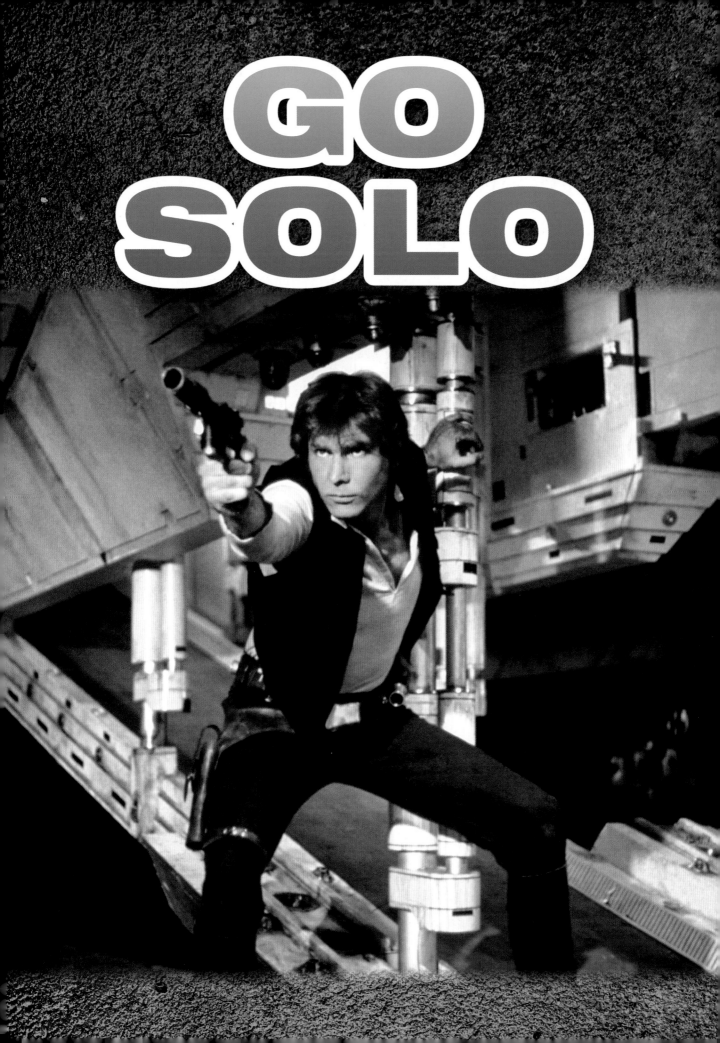

TAKE THE SHOT.

SORRY ABOUT
THE MESS.

TRY DOING THE RIGHT THING....
YOU MIGHT LIKE IT.

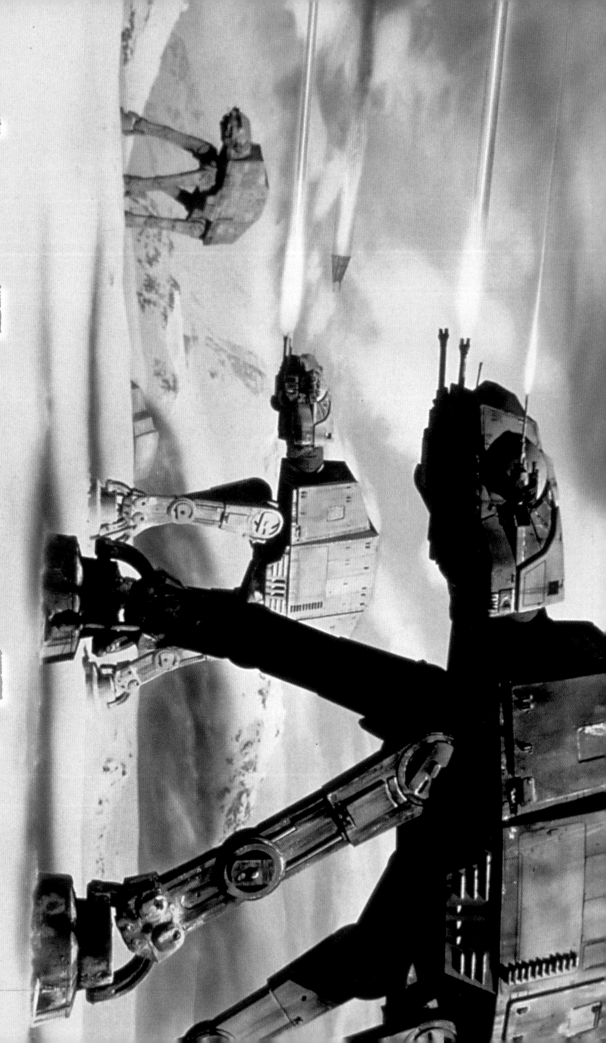

ALL-TERRAIN TERROR

As
Good
as Gold

You must learn the ways of the Force.

DUEL!

REBEL LEADERS

EVERY OBSTACLE HAS
A THERMAL EXHAUST PORT.

R2-D2

A good man is hard to find.

I am altering the deal. Pray I don't alter it any further.

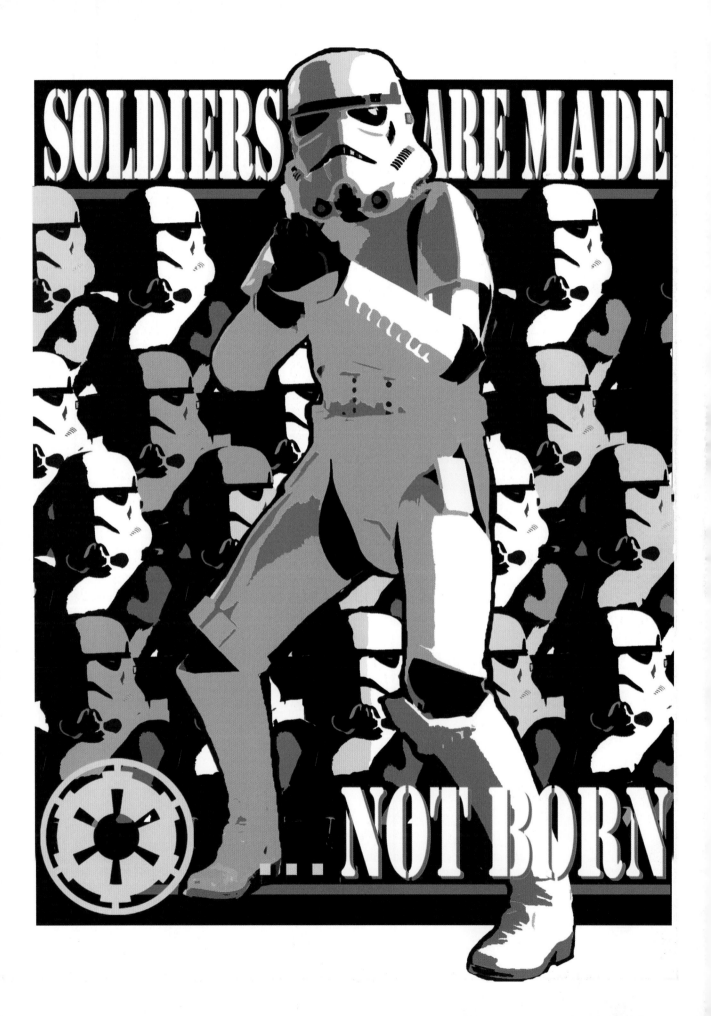

SHOCK AND AWE

RULE THE GALAXY

BOBA FETT
BOUNTY HUNTER

FURR-OCIOUS!

JUDGE ME BY MY SIZE, DO YOU?

HEROES SOMETIMES REQUIRE DETAILING.

NOWHERE
TO RUN.
NOWHERE
TO HIDE.

JOIN ME

BACK IN BLACK

Boba Fett? Where?

GOOD LUCK. YOU'RE GOING TO NEED IT.

SHORT HELP IS BETTER THAN NO HELP AT ALL.

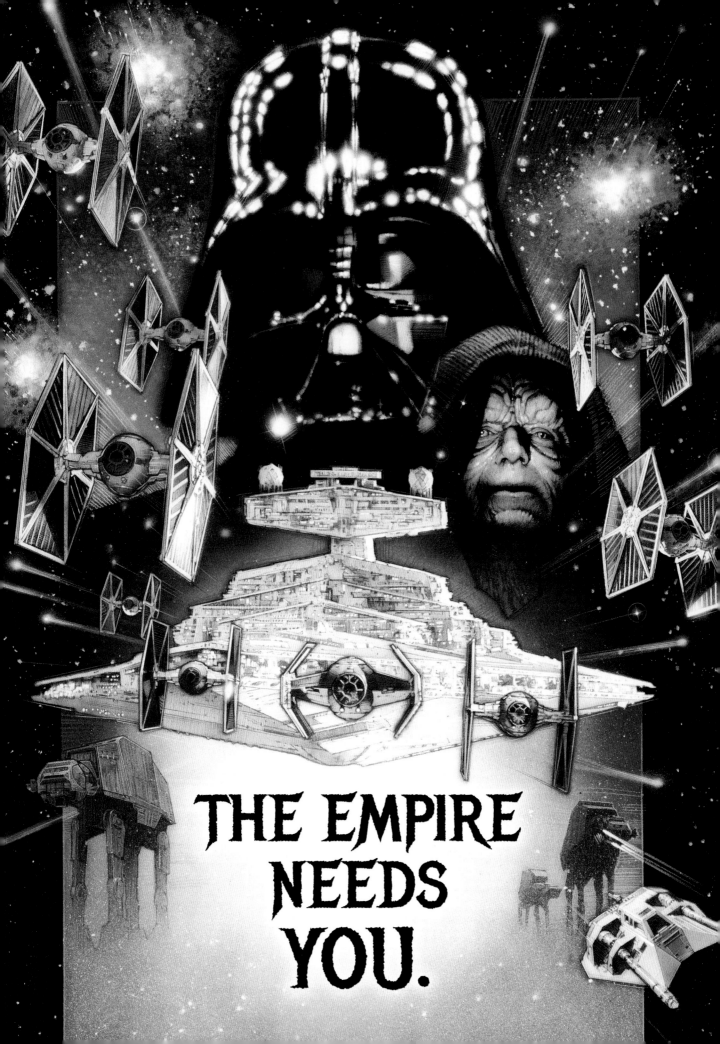

HEROES
AND
VILLAINS
COLLIDE

SOME THINGS ARE WORTH FIGHTING FOR.

REDEMPTION
HAPPENS

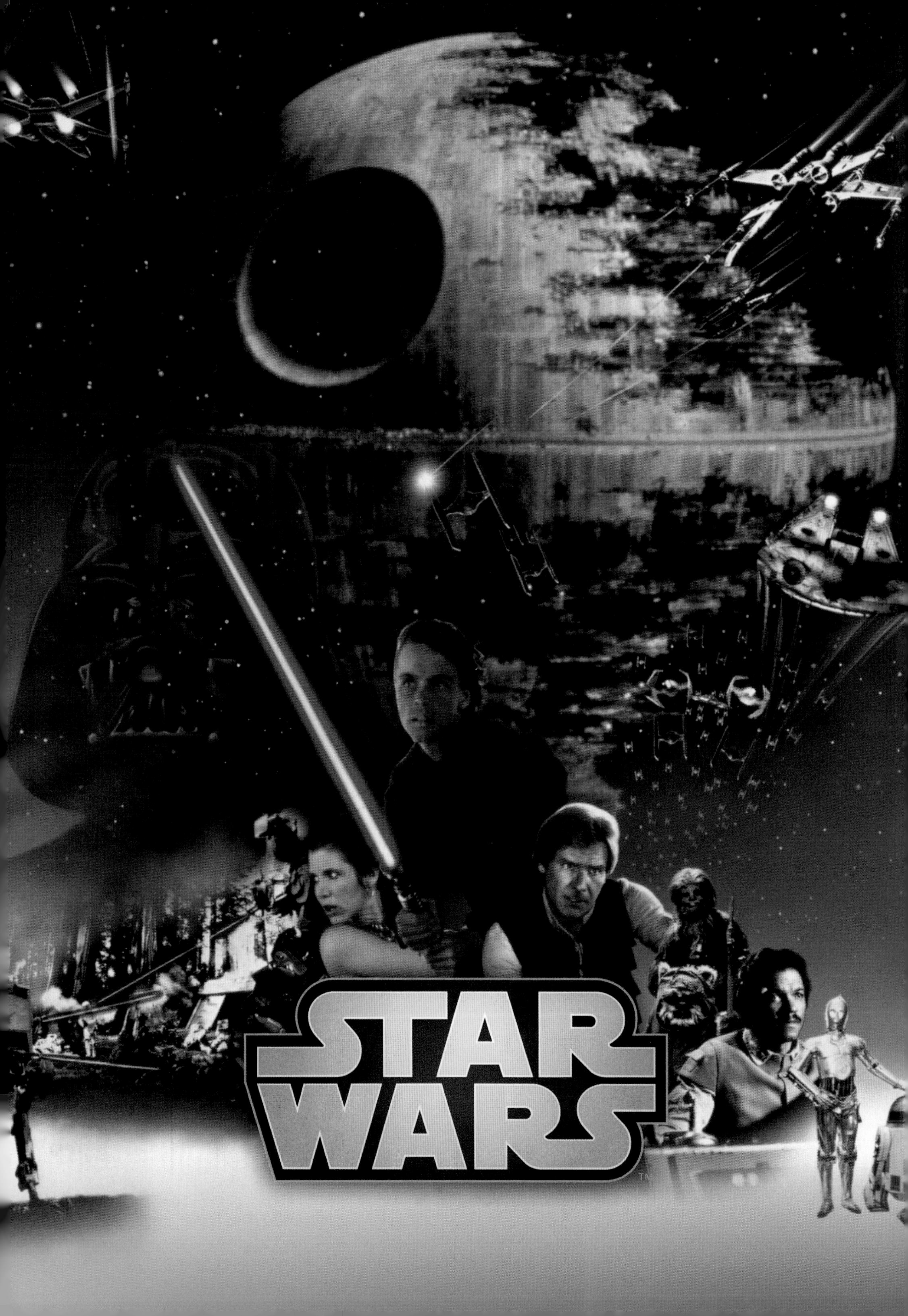
STAR WARS